P9-BHY-225

Island Morning

Written by **Rachna Gilmore**
Art by **Brenda Jones**

The Acorn Press
Charlottetown
2015

ACORNPRESS

P.O. Box 22024
Charlottetown, Prince Edward Island
C1A 9J2
acornpresscanada.com

Printed in Canada
Edited by Sherie Hodds
Designed by Matt Reid

Library and Archives Canada Cataloguing in Publication

Gilmore, Rachna, 1953-, author
Island morning / written by Rachna Gilmore ; art by Brenda Jones.

ISBN 978-1-927502-51-8 (bound)

I.Jones, Brenda, 1953-, illustrator II.Title.

PS8563.I57I84 2015   jC813'.54   C2015-904408-1

The publisher acknowledges the support of the Government of Canada through the Canada Book Fund of the Department of Canadian Heritage, the Canada Council of the Arts Block Grant Program and the support of the Province of Prince Edward Island.

For Ian, and for Rian
-RG

To Merlin, who makes all our
walks together inspiring
-BJ

In the still of the morning, the chill of the morning, we tiptoe outside, Grandpa and I.

The sun isn't up, but the sky whispers light. Everything is hushed and the grass is shivery with dew. There's no one about. Just the seagulls, swooping and gliding over the water, swooping and gliding.

The red lane pulls our feet up towards the cliff
edge. We weave through a narrow path as the
wind stirs and sighs. Branches whip-flap against
my legs. Wild grasses sway and drip. Before we
reach the cliff my pants are soaked with dew.

At the edge of the cliff, we stand for a
moment, Grandpa and I. The water is sleepy
this morning. It murmurs against the red shore.

Shush-flap. Shush-flap.

We turn and walk along the path,
towards the highest part of the cliff.

The sky becomes lighter and lighter. Then it turns to gold and the sun rises like fire on the water. The sky turns blue, blue, and the water smiles, so glad and wide. I open my arms to take it all in. Take in all that blue.

The wind picks up, teasing and fluffing my hair.

On we go, along the narrow path, up, up, up the slope to the fence at the top of the cliff.

The cows are on the other side, large, and lazy.

One comes to the fence and looks at us with big
hairy eyes. Her mouth sways sideways as she chews
and stares, chews and stares. The other cows come too,
one by one, until they all stand staring over the fence.

Grandpa takes off his cap and bows.
"Good day, ladies," he says.

I giggle and bow too.

The ladies just look at us, eyes wide, unimpressed.

Grandpa and I wave and go back down the path.

The chill of the morning lifts with the sun.
I unzip my jacket.

The still of the morning fills with bird cries and
the buzz and chirp of insects.

Down, down we go along the path,
right down to the beach.

The wind perks up and the waves go
slurp-dash, burp-dash.

We stand silently, Grandpa and I, and just take it in.

At last we turn and go back along the red lane to our house, our white house, shining like a shell in the sun.

Outside the front door, we stop. Just to hold on to the stillness a bit longer.

I squeeze Grandpa hand. It's large and rough. And quiet.

Then we go inside to the brisk smell of toast, the
sizzle of eggs and the chuckle and chortle of bacon
frying...to the hustle and bustle of the waking day.